My Backpack

by Iris Littleman
illustrated by Hector Borlasca

 HOUGHTON MIFFLIN HARCOURT
School Publishers

Copyright © by Houghton Mifflin Harcourt Publishing Company

Printed in China

ISBN-13: 978-0-547-01957-4
ISBN-10: 0-547-01957-2

9 10 11 0940 18 17 16 15 14 13
4500443494

book

See my book.

pencil

See my pencil.

apple

See my apple.

See my ball.

See my backpack!

Responding

✔ **TARGET SKILL** **Understanding Characters** Who is the main character in this story? What is he doing?

Talk About It

Text to World Draw a picture that shows a boy or girl getting ready for school. Talk about your picture.

✔ WORDS TO KNOW

like

✔ TARGET SKILL **Understanding Characters** Tell more about characters.

✔ TARGET STRATEGY **Infer/Predict** Use text clues to figure out more about story parts.

GENRE **Fiction** is a story that is made up.